HALF A MAN

For Eric Pearce, whose extraordinary
courage inspired this story. One of the
very last of McIndoe's "Guinea Pigs".

M. M.

For Paul, Anne, Kirsty and Lorna

G. O'C.

HALF A MAN
MICHAEL MORPURGO

ILLUSTRATED BY GEMMA O'CALLAGHAN

WALKER
BOOKS

WHEN I WAS VERY LITTLE, MORE THAN HALF A CENTURY AGO NOW, I USED TO HAVE NIGHTMARES. You don't forget nightmares. This one was always the same. It began with a face, a twisted, tortured face that screamed silently, a face without hair or eyebrows, a skull more than a face, a skull which was covered in puckered, scarred skin stretched over the cheekbones. It was Grandpa's face and he was staring at me out of his scream. And always the face was on fire, flames licking out of his ears and mouth.

I remember I always tried to force myself to wake

up, so that I wouldn't have to endure the rest of it. But I knew every time that the rest would follow however hard I tried to escape – that my nightmare would not release me, would not allow me to wake until the whole horrible tale had played itself out.

I saw a great ship ablaze on the ocean. There were men on fire jumping overboard as she went down, then swimming in a sea where the water burned and boiled around them. I saw Grandpa swimming towards a lifeboat, but it was packed with sailors and there was no room for Grandpa. He begged them to let him on, but they wouldn't. Behind him, the ship's bow lifted out of the sea, and the whole ship groaned like a wounded beast in her death throes. Then she went down, slipping slowly under the waves, gasping great gouts of steam in the last of her agony. A silence came over the burning sea. Grandpa was clinging to the lifeboat now, his elbows

hooked over the side. That was when I realized that I was in the lifeboat with the other sailors. He saw me looking down at him and reached out his hand for help. It was a hand with no fingers.

I would wake up then, shaking in my terror and knowing even now that my nightmare was not over. For my nightmare would always seem to happen just a day or two before Grandpa came to stay. It was a visit I always dreaded. He didn't come to see us in London very often, every couple of years at most, and usually at Christmas. Thinking about it now, I suppose this was part of the problem. There were perfectly good reasons why we

didn't and couldn't see more of him. He lived far away, on the Isles of Scilly, so it was a long way for him to come, and expensive too. Besides which,  he hated big cities like London. I'm sure if I'd seen him more often, I'd have got used to him – used to his face and his hands and his silent, uncommunicative ways.

I don't blame my mother and father. I can see now why they were so tense before each visit. Being as taciturn and unsmiling as he was, Grandpa can't have been an easy guest. But, even so, they did make it a lot worse for me than they needed to. Just before Grandpa came there were always endless warnings, from Mother in particular (he was my grandpa on my mother's side), about how I mustn't upset him, how I mustn't leave my toys lying about on the sitting-room floor because

he didn't see very well and might trip over them, how I mustn't have the television on too much because Grandpa didn't like noise. But most of all they drummed into me again and again that whatever I did, I must not under any circumstances stare at him – that it was rude, that he hated people staring at him, particularly children.

I tried not to; I tried very hard. When he first arrived I would always try to force myself to look at something else. Once I remember it was a Christmas decoration, a red paper bell hanging just above his head in the front hall. Sometimes I would make myself look very deliberately at his waistcoat perhaps, or the gold watch chain he always wore. I'd fix my gaze on anything just as long as it was nowhere near the forbidden places, because I knew that once I started looking at his forbidden face or his forbidden hands I wouldn't be able to stop myself.

But every time, sooner or later, I'd do it; I'd sneak a crafty look. And very soon that look became a stare. I was never at all revolted by what I saw. If I had been, I could have looked away easily. I think I was more fascinated than anything else, and horrified too, because I'd been told something of what had happened to him in the war. I saw the suffering he had gone through in his deep blue eyes – eyes that hardly ever blinked, I noticed. Then I'd feel my mother's eyes boring into me, willing me to stop staring, or my father would kick me under the table. So I'd look at Grandpa's waistcoat – but I could only manage it for a while. I couldn't help myself. I had to look again at the forbidden places. He had three half-fingers on one hand and no fingers at all on the other. His top lip had almost completely disappeared and one of his ears was little more than a hole in his head.

As I grew up I'd often ask about how exactly it had happened. My mother and father never seemed to want to tell me much about it. They claimed they didn't know any more than they'd told me already – that Grandpa had been in the merchant navy in the Second World War, that his ship had been torpedoed in the Atlantic, and he'd been terribly burnt. He'd been adrift in a boat for days and days, they told me, before he'd been picked up. He'd spent the rest of the war in a special hospital.

Every time I looked at his face and hands the story seemed to want to tell itself again in my head. I so much wanted to know more. And I wanted to know more about my grandmother, too, but that was a story that made everyone even more tight-lipped. I knew she was called Annie, but I had never met her and no one ever talked about her. All anyone would ever say was that she had "gone away" a very long time ago, before I was born. I longed to ask Grandpa himself about his ship being torpedoed, about my grandmother too, but I never dared, not even when I was older and got to know him a lot better.

I must have been about twelve when I first went to see him on my own on the Scilly Isles for my summer holiday, and by then the nightmares had gone. That's not to say I wasn't still apprehensive in those first few days after I arrived. But I was always happy to be there, happy

just to get out of London. I'd go and stay with him in his cottage on Bryher – a tiny island, only about eighty people live there. He had no electricity, only a generator in a shed outside, which he'd switch off before he went to bed. The cottage wasn't much more than a shed, either.

It was a different world for me and I loved it. He lived by himself and lived simply. The place smelt of warm damp and paraffin oil and fish – we had fish for almost every meal. He made some kind of living out of catching lobsters and crabs. How he managed to go fishing with his hands as they were I'll never know. But he did.

It was years before I discovered why he never smiled. It was because he couldn't. It was too painful. The skin simply wouldn't stretch. When he laughed, which wasn't often, it was always with a straight face. And when he smiled it was with his eyes only. I'd never understood that when I was little. His eyes were the same blue as the sea around Scilly on a fine day. He was silent,

I discovered, because he liked to keep himself to himself. I'm a bit the same, so I didn't mind. He wasn't at all unkind or morose, just quiet. He'd read a lot in the evenings, for hours, anything about boats – Arthur Ransome, C. S. Forester and Patrick O'Brian. He didn't have a television, so I'd read them too. I think I must have read every book Arthur Ransome wrote during my holidays on Scilly.

During the day he'd let me do what I liked. I could run free. I'd wander the island all day; I'd go climbing on the rocks on Samson Hill or Droppy Nose Point. I'd go swimming in Rushy Bay, shrimping off Green Bay. But as I got older he'd ask me to go out fishing with him more and more. He liked the company, I think, or maybe it was because he needed the help, even if he never said so. I'd catch wrasse and pollock for baiting his lobster pots. I'd help him haul them in and extract

the catch. We would work almost silently together, our eyes meeting from time to time. Sometimes he'd catch me staring at him as he had when I was little. All those years later and I still couldn't help myself. But now it was different. Now all the fear had gone. Now I knew him well enough to smile at him when our eyes met, and, as I was later to find out, he understood perfectly well why I was staring at him, at his forbidden face, his forbidden hands.

It wasn't until the summer I just left school that Grandpa first told me himself about what had happened to him when his ship went down. He talked more these days, but never as much as the day we saw the gannets. We were out in his fishing boat. We'd picked up the pots, caught a few mackerel for supper, and were coming back in a lumpy sea round the back of Bryher, when a pair of gannets flew over and dived together, spearing the sea

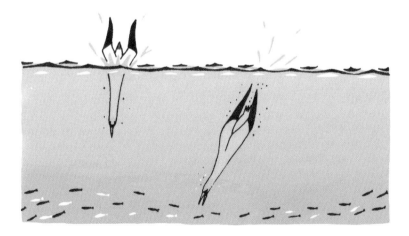

just ahead of us. "See that, Grandpa?" I cried. "Aren't they brilliant?"

"Better than brilliant," he said. "They bring you good luck, you know."

We watched the gannets surface, swallow their catch and take off again. We caught each other's eye and smiled, enjoying the moment together.

"You know what I like about you, Michael?" he went on. "You look at me. Most people don't. Your mother doesn't, and she's my own daughter. She looks away. Most people look away. Not that I blame them. I did once. Not any more. But you don't look away." He smiled. "You've been having sneaky old looks at me ever since you were knee-high to a grasshopper. If you looked away it was only to be polite, I always knew that. You've always wanted to ask me, haven't you? You wanted to know, didn't you? How this happened, I mean."

He touched his face. "I never told anyone before, not your mother, not even Annie. I just told them what they needed to know and no more, that my ship went down and after a few days in a lifeboat I got picked up. That's all I said. The rest they could see for themselves." He was looking straight ahead of him,

steering the boat as he was talking.

"I was a handsome enough devil before that – looked a bit like you do now. Annie and me got married a couple of years before the war broke out. A year later, I was in the merchant navy, in a convoy coming back from America. My third trip, it was." He looked

out towards Scilly Rock and wiped his face with the back of his hand. "It was a day like this, the day we copped it – the day I became half a man. Early evening, it happened. I'd seen ships go down before, dozens of them, and every time I thanked God it wasn't me. Now it was my turn.

"I was on watch when the first torpedo struck. Never saw it coming. The first hit us amidships. The second blew off the stern – took it right off. All hell broke loose. A great ball of fire came roaring through the ship,

set me on fire and cooked me like a sausage. Jim – Jim Channing, he came from Scilly too, him and me were mates, always were, even at school, joined up together – he smothered the flames, put them out. Then he helped me to the side. I'd never even have got that far without Jim. He made me jump. I didn't want to, because the sea was on fire. But he made me. He had hold of me and swam me away from the ship, so's we wouldn't get sucked down, he said. He got me to a lifeboat. There were too many in it already and they didn't want us."

I could see it! I could see it in my head. It was straight out of my nightmare.

"Jim said that he could hang on to the side but I'd been burnt and they had to help me into the boat. In the end they did, and Jim clung on beside me, still in the water, and we talked. We had to talk, and keep talking, Jim told me, so we didn't go to sleep, because if we went to sleep, like as not we'd never wake up again. So we told each other all the stories we knew: *Peter Rabbit*, the *Just So Stories* – anything we could remember. When we ran out of stories, we tried singing songs instead: 'Ten Green Bottles', 'Oranges and Lemons', anything. Time and again I dropped off to sleep, but Jim would always wake me up. Then one time I woke and Jim just wasn't there. He was gone. I've thought about Jim every day of my life since, but I've never spoken about him, until now.

"He's out there, Michael. Jim's out there, down in the deep somewhere. They all are, all the lads that went down in that ship, good lads. And there's been plenty of times since, I can tell you, when I wished to God I'd gone down with them."

He said nothing more for a while. I'd never heard him talk like this before, never. But he hadn't finished yet.

"All we saw for days on end were gannets," he went on. "Except once we did see a whale, a ruddy great whale. But that was all. No ships. No aeroplanes. Nothing. Just sea and sky. Some of the lads were burnt even worse than I was. They didn't last long. We were out there on the open ocean for a week or more. No food, no water. I lost count of the days and the nights. By then I didn't know any more who was alive and who was dead, and what's more I didn't care. I only knew I was still alive. That was all that mattered to me. I lived on nothing but hope, and a dream. I had a dream and I clung on to it. I dreamt of getting back to Annie, of coming home. I thought if I dreamt it hard enough, hoped for it hard enough, it must come true.

"Then, one morning, I wake up and there's this huge destroyer right there alongside us and men looking down over the side and waving and shouting.

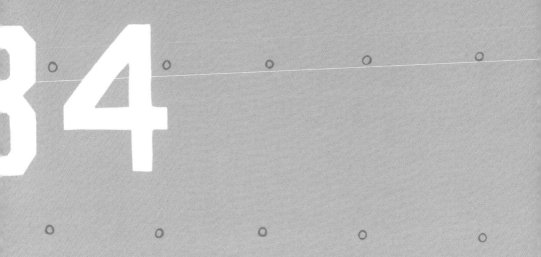

I thought I was still in my dream, but I wasn't. Only three of us out of that whole lifeboat survived. They patched me up as best they could, and shipped me home. The next thing I knew I was in this hospital, down in Sussex it was, East Grinstead. That's where they put the pieces of me together again, like a sort of jigsaw puzzle, but the pieces were skin and bone and flesh. The trouble was, there were some pieces of my jigsaw missing, so

they had a bit of a job, which is why I still look a bit of a mess. But I wasn't the worst in that hospital, not by a long shot.

"Dr McIndoe, he was called. Wonderful man he was, a genius. It was him that did it, put us back together, and I'm not just talking about the operations. He was a magician in the operating theatre, all right. But it's what he did afterwards for us. He made us feel right

again inside, like we mattered, like we weren't monster men. It was a hospital full of men like me, but mostly air-force boys. We were all together, every one of us patched up in one way or another, so it didn't matter what we looked like even when we went out and about. Everyone treated us right: nurses and doctors, everyone. Annie came to see me when she could. Right away I saw she didn't look at me the same, didn't speak to

me like I was normal, like the nurses did. She still loved
me, I think, but all she saw was a monster man.

"After a while, when the war was over, I left the hospital and came home to Annie, home to Scilly. My dream had come true, I thought. But of course it hadn't. I soon found that out. Annie tried – tried her best. I tried too. We had a baby – your mother, Michael – but Annie still wasn't looking at me. I drank too much,

said things I shouldn't have said. She did too, told me I should stop feeling sorry for myself, that I wasn't the man she'd married any more. Then we just stopped talking to one another. One day I came back home from a day's fishing and she'd left, just like that, taking my little girl, your mother, with her. She'd had enough. I don't blame her, not any more. No one wants a monster for a husband. No one wants half a man, and that's what I was, Michael, half a man. That's what I still am. But I blamed her then. I hated her. Every day it was all I could think of, how much I hated her.

"I lived with that hate inside me most of my life. Hate, anger, call it what you will. It's like a cancer. It eats away at you. She wouldn't let me see my little girl, even when she was older. I never forgave her for that. She said I drank too much, which was true – said I'd frighten her too much. Maybe she was right. Maybe she was right."

It wasn't the moment to say anything, so I didn't. We fell into our silence again.

We unloaded the catch, moored the boat and walked together back home up the hill. We cooked the mackerel and sat eating it, still in silence. I was silent because I was reliving his story in my head. But I had one thing I needed to say.

"She wasn't right," I told him. "Annie should have let you see your own daughter. Everyone has a right to see their own child."

"Maybe," he replied. "But the truth is, I think I do frighten your mother a little, even now. So Annie was right, in her way. Your mother came to see me for the first time after she'd left school, when she wasn't a little girl any more; practically grown up, she was. She came without ever asking her mother, to find out who her father was, she said; because she hadn't ever known me,

not properly. She was kind to me. She's been kind to me ever since. But even now she can't look me in the eye like you do. She writes letters, keeps in touch, calls me Dad, lets me visit, does her best by me, always has. And I'm grateful, don't get me wrong. But every time I came to you for Christmas when you were little, I longed for her just to look at me. She wants to, but she can't. And she's angry, too, like I was. She can't forgive her mother for what she did, for taking her away from her dad. She hasn't spoken to her mother now in over twenty years. Time's come to forgive and forget; that's what I think."

So now I knew the whole story for the first time. We relapsed after that into our usual, quiet ways for the rest of the holidays. But by the time I left I think I was closer to him than I have ever been to anyone else in my life.

I went back a year later, this time with my mother, to visit him in hospital. He was already too ill to get out of bed. He said he was a lucky man because he could see the sea from his bed. He died the second night we were there. He'd left a letter for me on the mantelpiece in his cottage.

Dear Michael,

See they bury me at sea. I want to be with Jim and the others. I want Annie there, and I want your mother there too. I want you all there together. I want things put right. Thanks for looking at me like you did.

Love,
Grandpa

A few days later, Annie came over to Scilly for the funeral. She held hands with my mother as Grandpa's ashes were scattered out beyond Scilly Rock. Grandmother, mother and son, all of us together. We were lucky. We had a fine day for it. The gannets were flying, and everyone was together, just as Grandpa had wanted. So he was right about gannets. He was right about a lot of things.

But he wasn't half a man.